This
Wickleville Storybook
proudly belongs to

_____

another Wickleville pal!

The Wickleville Fair
©2000 by TREND enterprises, Inc.
Wickleville Woods™ is a trademark of TREND enterprises, Inc.

Printed in the United States of America

Lynae Wingate, John R. Kober – Editors

Library of Congress Catalog Card Number: 99-69465

ISBN 1-889319-71-6

10 9 8 7 6 5 4 3 2

The Wickleville Fair

by Jeffrey Sculthorp

Illustrations by Lorin Walter

WICKLEVILLE WOODS™

TREND enterprises, Inc.

It was time for the annual Wickleville Fair.

All of the animals were going to be there.

All of the chipmunks, squirrels, and even the dogs

would be there with the birds, rabbits, cats, and the frogs.

It was Murphy the mouse's first ever big fair.

He was ready for fun with best friend, Buzzy the bear.

Murphy was amazed at so many things to see and to ride,

7

especially the water park with a one-hundred-foot slide.

Exhibits

Murphy wanted to go on every ride at the fair,

even the Twirl 'n Whirl, if Buzzy would dare.

They went into the Fun House with silly, painted clowns;

and into a room that turned
everything upside down.

Then Murphy and Buzzy were excited to find,

the Clam Cup Roller Coaster—a one of a kind.

14

But Buzzy got scared to ride the clams filled with sand.

So Murphy made it better and held Buzzy's hand.

They jumped in the roller coaster, about to have a blast.

Just then Rascal Raccoon stepped up and said, "Wait! Not so fast!"

"Sorry Murphy, you're not tall enough to go on these rides.

You can't ride the roller coaster or one-hundred-foot slide."

But Buzzy had another idea up his sleeve.

There was a solution; Murphy did not have to leave.

Buzzy picked up Murphy and he started to run...

to a place Buzzy knew that they both would have fun.

Murphy the mouse
could not help that he was not any taller.

So, they still went on rides. . .

WICKLEVILLE
FAIR
KIDDIE PARK

but the rides were just a bit smaller.

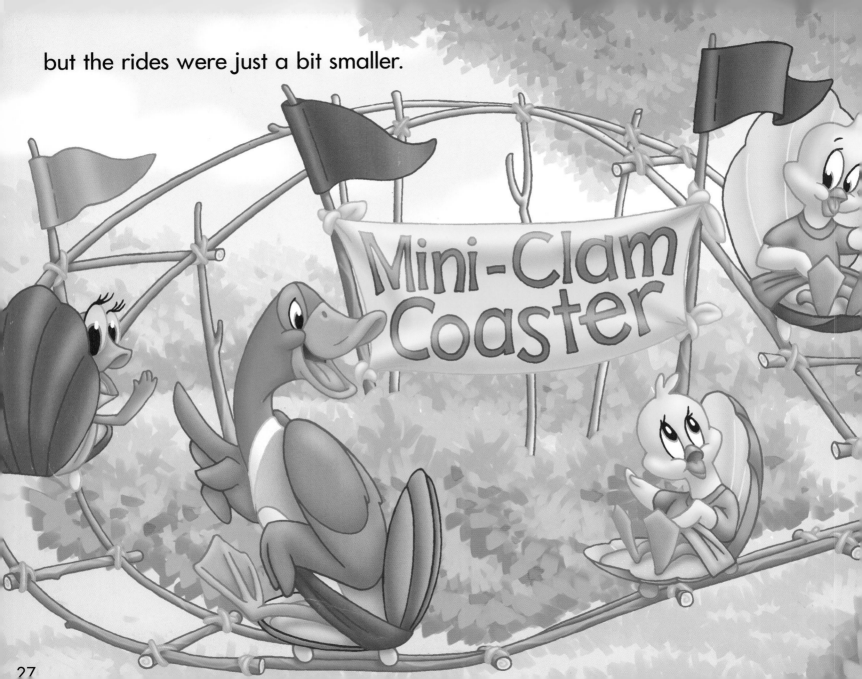

Mini-Clam Coaster